CHRISTMAS PUDS & KILLERS

CHRISTIAN COZY MYSTERY

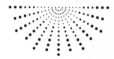

DONNA DOYLE

CONTENTS

INTRODUCTION

A PERSONAL WORD FROM PUREREAD

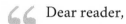 Dear reader,

Do you love a good mystery? So do we! Nothing is more pleasing than a page turner that keeps you guessing until the very last page.

In our Christian cozy mysteries you can be certain that there won't be any gruesome or gory scenes, swearing or anything else upsetting, just good clean fun as you unravel the mystery together with our marvelous characters.

Thank you for choosing PureRead!

A Warm Welcome From Donna Doyle

PUREREAD
CLEAN READS
FOR PURE HEARTS

To find out more about PureRead mysteries and receive new release information and other goodies from Donna Doyle go to our website
PureRead.com/donnadoyle

~

Enjoy The Story!

A TIME OF CHEER

"What do you think? Is this centered?" Sammy got off the stepladder and stood back to admire her work. The massive green wreath Johnny had dragged out of the storage area looked wonderful on the wall behind the counter, complemented by the strands of evergreen garland and the big red bows that held it up. The snow was falling thickly outside, making the warm interior of Just Like Grandma's feel incredibly cozy.

"Looks great to me," Helen said with a smile. "I don't think I've seen the diner look this good in years. Every time Christmas comes rolling around, I think about getting all those decorations back out. But I get busy and it never happens. Just where do you come up with all your energy, anyway?"

Sammy shrugged as she moved the stepladder a few feet down and picked up a little Santa statue that would fit perfectly on a shelf on the wall. "I don't know. I think I'm just determined to enjoy the holidays this year. They were so awful the last few years when I was still with Greg. I fooled myself into thinking I was having fun while I tagged along to his company Christmas parties and watched him flirt with all the women, when what I really wanted to do was volunteer at the soup kitchen or even just spend some time with my Bible and celebrate the birth of Jesus."

"I take it he wasn't a Christian man?"

"Not exactly." Sammy shook her head at the memories, wondering how she had ever managed to get herself into a relationship like that. All the trauma with her father's arrest had driven her away from the religion of her childhood, but had that really been an excuse? Even if it wasn't, at least she finally had a chance to make things right again. "I think going to church every Sunday has really helped me get into the spirit of things."

"Pastor Mike has a way of doing that to people," Helen agreed as she pulled a package of ornaments out of a nearby box. "You think we should put a tree up? I have a six-footer somewhere."

"Sure, why not? We can set it up over by the table of baked goods so it won't be in the way. I think it'll look nice. But I think I need to be done with this for now. We're starting to get some customers coming in, and if they go as crazy for my gingerbread cookies as I hope they will, I'll need to get a new batch in the over soon." She put away her decorating mess and washed her hands.

Several customers had just come in looking for breakfast, and they sat at a table in the front corner. The group consisted of four older women, and they sat talking together like school girls in the cafeteria.

"What can I get for you ladies this morning?"

"There she is!" said one of them with excitement, her sparkly earrings shaking with excitement. "Make sure you get one of her biscuits, Maureen. You've never tasted anything better!"

"I have already had the biscuits, Linda," replied her friend next to her. This woman had hair that was dyed a very deep shade of brown that couldn't possibly have been natural, and it was cut in a bob at her chin. "As well as her cinnamon rolls, and her dinner rolls, and her cookies, and her pecan pie. That's exactly why we're here, isn't it?"

Sammy tapped the end of her pen on her chin and smiled. She had no idea what they were talking about, except that it involved her. "Is there something I can help you with?"

Maureen, the dark-haired one, nodded her head and folded her hands primly on the table in front of her. "Yes, dear. We're the Radical Grandmas. I take it you've heard of us?"

Glancing across the diner at Helen and wondering just who these interesting ladies were, Sammy shook her head. "I'm sorry, I can't say that I have."

"Then you haven't been getting out enough," Maureen asserted. "You see, we do a lot for this community. If there's a fundraiser, a coat drive, a trivia night, or a craft fair in Sunny Cove, then we've had a hand in it. And right now, we're organizing a fundraiser to save to Sunny Cove Recreation Center."

"That's wonderful," Sammy enthused, not even having been aware that the rec center needed saving. "If you'd like to leave a flyer with me, I can ask Helen about putting it up near the counter where people can see it."

"We were actually hoping that you could do much more for us than that," smiled a woman with a blonde pouf of hair on top of her head. "I'm Agnes Miller, by the way."

Sammy shook the hand the older woman held out, finding it cool and soft. "It's very nice to meet you."

"Oh, you poor thing!" laughed the fourth woman as she slapped a hand on the table. "You look like you think you might get abducted by aliens or something! We just wanted to see if you could do some baking for us. It's going to be a big Christmas party, you see."

"You never could stand the suspense, could you Viola?" snapped Maureen. She turned a smile to Sammy. "But she's right. We'd like a big, glorious Christmas cake to raffle off. We know what a reputation you have around here for your baked goods, and we think it will bring in quite a bit of money. There will also be a per plate charge for everyone who's joining us for dinner, and some local businesses are bringing in items for a silent auction."

Sammy had to smile. It sounded like a big task, but she

was always up for helping a worthy cause. It would take her some time in the kitchen, but baking was what she was good at. "Sure, I'd love to help."

"Don't say that just yet," Agnes cautioned, her gold bangle bracelets jingling as she shook a warning finger at Sammy. "You haven't heard all of it."

"No?" Even though the diner had just opened, Sammy already knew these were her most interesting customers of the day.

"No," Maureen affirmed. "We really want to create the effect of an old-fashioned, community Christmas. We need about eight to ten Christmas puddings as well. We're happy to pay for materials—we know you have to spend money to make money—but we're hoping you'd be willing to donate your time."

Sammy stared at them for a moment, her mouth open. "Um," she finally said when she shut it again, "I'm afraid I've never made a Christmas pudding before."

"Oh, you'll do just fine at it, dear," Agnes insisted. "I've watched a few cooking shows about this sort of thing, and it doesn't really seem all that hard, especially with your talent."

"They're sort of like fruit cakes, only rounder and tastier," Viola volunteered. "I'm sure there are some cookbooks down at the library that can help. I might not work there anymore, but I still know that place like the back of my hand. I can point you right to them."

Maureen shook her head. "She doesn't need your dusty old books, Viola. She'll just look them up on the internet like all the young kids do these days."

"Everyone needs books, dusty or not," Viola argued.

Sammy would have thought the ladies were having a genuine argument, but she noted the sparkle in their eyes as they spoke to each other. Clearly, the relationship between the four of them was one that had been forged over many years, and they were comfortable enough with each other to tease a little. "I'll see what I can do. When is the fundraiser? And where?"

"December seventeenth at the rec center," Maureen explained. "Does that mean we can count on your help?"

"Of course. Do you have any certain flavors or themes in mind?" She had been poised to write down their order, but instead she began jotting down her projects for the fundraiser. She could already see the Christmas cake in her mind.

"Just one requirement: no nuts. I have an allergy, and we know quite a few other people do these days."

Sammy wrote their wish in big, bold letters at the bottom of the ticket. "Not a problem."

Once she had their contact information and everything was settled, they finally placed their order. Sammy took the ticket to the back to give to Johnny, and Helen joined her. "That was quite a conversation just for some waffles and biscuits."

"Oh, it was much more than that!" Sammy replied excitedly. "They want me to do some baked goods to help with their fundraiser for the rec center. It sounds like a great cause, and it will bring in some publicity for the diner, too."

"And it'll be a nice showcase for your talents," Helen reminded her. "Not that you need it. They never would have asked you for something like that if they didn't already know just how good you are."

"I don't know about that. They want a huge cake and several Christmas puddings, the latter of which I've never made. I don't know how well they'll turn out." Sammy's excitement had overwhelmed her logic, and she was now seriously wondering if she could pull this off. "I'm going to have to do a lot of research on this one."

"Even so, the Radical Grandma's don't do anything halfway. If they didn't think you could do it, they wouldn't have even considered you. You should be flattered." Helen threw her gray braid over her shoulder and patted Sammy on the back. "They have confidence in you, and you should have some in yourself."

"Thanks," Sammy said with a smile. "For now, it looks like I need to get some more biscuits going. I've heard the door ding several times, and all that Christmas decorating put me behind for the breakfast rush."

2

CHRISTMAS PUDDINGS

Three days later, Sammy stood in the kitchen of Just Like Grandma's well after the diner had closed. Johnny had gone home for the day, as had Helen once she had wished Sammy luck. "I have no doubt you'll do well, Sammy my dear," she said with a wink as she headed out the back door.

Unfortunately, Sammy wasn't quite so certain. She had met up with Viola at the Sunny Cove Library, where the older woman instantly led her to a section of cookbooks that were just as dusty as Maureen had said they would be. Sammy had checked several out and spent hours looking through them and learning about Christmas puddings as well as several other old-fashioned recipes that she would like to try. Then, she had spent some time on the internet, watching videos about how to bake the Christmas puddings and finding so many recipes she wasn't sure which ones to try first. Some of this was dictated by the ingredients that each one called for, since some of them weren't available in Sunny Cove. Even a trip to the larger grocery store over in Oak Hills hadn't been quite enough, and some of the puddings would have to wait until the order she placed online came in. Still, she could get started on a few of the recipes.

"Okay, Sammy. Your last name isn't Baker for nothing," she said to herself as she took the plastic wrap off a bowl of dried fruit she had left to soak the night before. "People have been making these things for centuries, and there's no reason you can't do it now."

But the fact remained that this was something new to her, and it definitely wasn't the same as a typical cake or yeast bread. Sammy was just about to start adding the rest of the ingredients when she heard a knocking sound from the front of the diner. She paused, thinking she was hearing things because she wasn't used to being in Just Like Grandma's after hours, but then the knocking came again.

With a sigh, Sammy headed through the swinging door and into the dining room, prepared to tell whoever had been rude enough to come by that they weren't open and to come back in the morning. But she recognized the face peering in the glass of the front door, with his wild black hair sticking out from under a striped stocking cap, and she unlocked the door. "Austin, what are you doing out so late?"

"I went for a walk," he informed her with a proud smile. "Walking reduces fat and lowers blood pressure."

Considering that the poor boy had spent some of his life scrounging in dumpsters, Sammy doubted that he needed to worry about body fat. She shut and locked the door behind him. "What about your Uncle Mitch? Does he know where you are?" Austin lived with his uncle, not having any other family, and the old man often had a hard time keeping up with his rambunctious nephew. Austin was a grown man in his early twenties, but he had the energy of a twelve-year-old.

"He's asleep," Austin replied. "Do we have any jobs?"

Sammy had been helping Austin earn a little money around town by lining up jobs where he could pick up trash or rake leaves. It was a lot of work for her, as well, but it kept Austin from getting in trouble for stealing. "Not right now, I don't. All the leaves have been taken care of, and it's awful cold outside. Once the snow starts falling, though, we can have you shovel some sidewalks."

"Okay."

It was the shortest thing Sammy had ever heard coming out of his mouth, and she could see some of the light go out of his dark eyes. "Hey, it's just for a little while. Besides, I've got a whole bunch of things to bake for a fundraiser. You can help me for a few minutes while you warm up from the cold, and then I'll take you home." She led him into the back.

She had asked Helen once before if Austin could have a job in the kitchen, but the older woman had said she'd tried it before without success. Sammy had been working with Austin for a few months now, and she was hopeful that the result would be different. He was comfortable around her, and she was patient enough with him that he didn't get out of control. "First, you need to take off your coat and hat. You can hang them right there on the peg."

He did as he was told, even if he moved slowly. "What are we making?"

"Christmas pudding."

"I like pudding, especially pistachio," Austin enthused as Sammy directed him to the sink to wash his hands.

"This is a different kind of pudding," she explained. "It's more like a dense cake with lots of fruit in it."

"Is it good?"

"Well, I haven't tried it yet. We'll have to find out." Sammy tied an apron onto Austin and brought him over to the counter, where she had measured out most of the ingredients. "Okay, see that bowl of spices? You can dump that whole thing into this bowl of dried fruit."

"It looks funny," he said as he took a sniff. "And it smells funny, too."

"The fruit has been soaked in brandy overnight," Sammy explained. "But there are other ways of doing it, as well. I have another bowl that's been soaked in tea, and one that's been soaked in orange juice. I want to see which ones work the best." She had determined from her research that the ones made with alcohol were the most traditional and would probably taste the best, but she didn't want anyone at the fundraiser to be offended. The alcohol would cook off during the steaming process, but still.

Austin continued to add ingredients and mix at her direction. He was greasing the pudding mold when something occurred to her. "Austin, what are you and Uncle Mitch doing for Christmas? Do you celebrate at home? Or go to church?"

He stuck the tip of his tongue out while he finished pouring the batter into the mold. "My cousin Rachel said she wants to have a big family dinner, so we're going over there and going to church with her."

She hadn't realized just how worried she had been about this. Austin and his uncle were good people who simply had been handed a rough lot in life, and she hated to think of the two of them sitting in their trailer without having a real holiday. "Where does your cousin live?"

"I don't know. Uncle Mitch will drive."

"I'm sure he will." Sammy was busy boiling water on the stove and making sure the pan was ready for steaming. "I think that's about done. Here, it's time to pour the pudding in. Hold the mold still for me. Now I'll let you push it all down with the spoon to get the air bubbles out."

"What are you doing?" he asked as she pleated a piece of parchment paper and put it and a sheet of aluminum foil over the top of the bowl.

The strangest part—even to Sammy—was when she tied a string around the bowl to make a handle. "The traditional way to cook a pudding is by steaming it on the stove. I put a saucer in the bottom of this pan so the pudding won't touch the bottom, and then I'll pour in hot water. We'll turn it on, like this, and cover it. The steam will cook it."

Austin watched, mesmerized. "I've seen Uncle Mitch put a lasagna in the oven before. I guess he forgot the water."

Sammy laughed at his innocence. "Not everything is cooked this way. It's just the best way for puddings. But I read you can also do it in the oven, in a slow cooker, or in a pressure cooker, but there's always steam involved."

"So there's lots of different kinds?" he asked, peering through the glass lid on the pot.

"It seems to be that way. Different fruits, different liquids, different kinds of sugar, and different ways to cook it. And heaven help me, but I want to try them all." Her first experiment smelled delicious already, and it had barely started cooking.

"Can I try some?"

"I'll be sure to save you one once they're done. Apparently, the longer they sit the better they taste. This one will need to cook for at least five hours, anyway. Come on, I'll take you home." As Sammy drove Austin back to his trailer park down by the river, she felt a warmth in her heart at knowing she had made a special Christmas dish with him. He was such a sweet person, and he deserved all the goodness in the world. She only wished she had remembered the tradition of everyone making a wish as they stirred the pudding. It would be interesting to see just what he would wish for.

Once he was safely inside, Sammy drove back to the diner to check the water level in the pot. It was fine, but she was going to be up half the night making sure it got done. She set an alarm on her phone to check it again in half an hour and started mixing up the next pudding.

3

MERRY AND BRIGHT

"T hat's the last of it." Sammy loaded the final pudding into the back of her RAV4. She had done her best to make sure everything was sealed and steady, including the massive cake, but the idea of bringing everything to the other side of town still made her nervous. She adjusted one place before closing the back gate and climbing behind the wheel.

"Don't look so nervous," Helen said from the passenger seat as she buckled her belt. "It's going to be wonderful."

"I hope you're right. I spent forever on those puddings. They take so long to cook! I tried so many different recipes that I ended up having to label them so I won't look like an idiot if someone asks me what's in a certain one. They're supposed to taste the best when they've sat for a while, so at least that means these should be even better than the ones I cut open and tried."

"You have nothing to worry about. And I saw that cake

you made. The guests are going to go nuts for it. I'll be interested to see just how much money the raffle brings in."

Fifteen minutes later, Sammy and Helen were unloading the giant cake from the car and bringing it in the back door of the Sunny Cove Recreation Center.

"Oh, right here!" Agnes ushered them into the bar and café area and showed them a table that had been set up exclusively for the cake raffle. The center remained clear for the showpiece, but the rest of it had been covered in garland and holly. A gold raffle drum stood off to the side. "That cake is just exquisite, Sammy! How did you ever get so much detail on it?"

Sammy was proud of herself as she set the cake down in the designated spot. "A lot of practice and the right tools," she replied honestly. She had spent plenty of time just designing the cake, deciding on a white frosting with white piping that looked like Christmas lace. She had added edible pearls and fondant holly. A close runner-up for ideas had been to decorate the cake to look like a winter scene, complete with evergreens, snowmen, and skiers, but the holly seemed more tradition and went along with the puddings.

"It looks as though you ladies have put quite a bit of effort into this event, as well," Helen said, admiring the candles in the centerpieces, the three-piece band, and the massive Christmas tree. "I feel like I've traveled in time."

"That was the idea!" Agnes beamed. "We thought it would

be nice to bring people out of modern times and remind them what the holidays used to be like. And this place means so much to us, we hope we can make it mean something to everyone else as well."

"Why is that, if I may ask?" Sammy had been wondering about this, but she had never found the right time to ask. "I mean, I'm not sure why the Radical Grandmas are so interested in the rec center."

"That's simple," Agnes replied with a twinkle in her eye. "When I retired, I didn't know what to do with myself anymore. My husband had passed away several years before that, and all my grandkids were grown and doing their own thing. I was just wasting away, when my doctor suggested I come out here and take a water aerobics class. I won't lie to you; I didn't want to come at first. But I knew it was best for my health."

"And it turns out," Viola said as she walked up and joined them, "that Agnes wasn't the only lonely old grandma with nothing to do. The four of us were all in that same class. Soon enough, we started chatting in the locker room. That led to going out for coffee afterwards, and before we knew it we were inseparable. We started working on projects of all sorts, and the Radical Grandmas began."

"That's just marvelous," Sammy replied honestly, feeling tears burn at the back of her eyes. "True friendships are hard to find, and everyone should be as lucky as the four of you."

"That's exactly why we have to fight to save this old place," Viola said seriously. "Sure, there are a few young kids who come in on weekends for swimming lessons, but a quick revamp could really pull in a crowd and ensure that the rec center stays open."

"I'm sure you'll achieve your goals tonight," Helen said, watching the first guests come trickling in the door. "We put up a few flyers in the diner, and I talked to quite a few customers who said they were interested. They'll be thrilled when they see how lovely it all is."

"I'm afraid not everyone is thrilled," Viola said with a frown as she glanced across the room. "Here comes Maureen, and she looks like she's on the warpath."

She certainly did. In a bright red satin dress with a puffed skirt, she looked like the perfect party hostess. But Maureen's fists were clenched at her sides, and her jaw was tight as she marched up to the little group. The forced smile on her face didn't reach her eyes. "I'm trying to understand why all the wait staff are wearing Santa suits," she grated out. "I don't remember anyone saying anything about that."

"I thought it was a nice touch," Agnes asserted. "And look, the children are going crazy for them already." She pointed to a family that had just been seated at a table by the window. Two young boys were clapping and pointing at the waiters as they brought their water glasses.

"But that's not what we discussed!" Maureen asserted.

"And it doesn't have the same traditional feel as everything else does!"

"Maureen, dear, I know you like everything just so, but I assure you it will be fine. Just look at the cake Sammy made. Do you think anyone is even going to look at the wait staff once they see this beauty?" Viola gave an apologetic glance to Agnes while directing Maureen's attention to the cake.

And it was pretty enough to make even someone like Maureen stop complaining. "Oh my." She stepped slowly toward the cake, admiring it. "Oh, that's just elegant. Sammy, you must truly have the spirit of God in you to be able to create something like that."

"That's got to be the best compliment I've ever received," Sammy replied warmly.

Maureen turned to Agnes with a smile. "I'm sorry I complained about your idea, honey. I've just been so worried about this fundraiser going right. You know how much this place means to us, and I think we just wouldn't be the same again if we didn't have it anymore."

The three women put their arms around each other and their heads together as they walked across the room, where Linda had just come in the door.

Helen nudged Sammy with her elbow. "Do you see what I see? The raffle drum is already filling up! They're selling the tickets for five dollars each, so just think of how much money they're making before this event even gets underway. You'll be the hero of the day, Sammy!"

With their job done, Sammy and Helen took their seats. It didn't take long before the party was in full swing. Every prominent member of the community had arrived, from business owners to politicians to teachers. Sammy was introduced to so many people that she was sure she would never remember their faces or their names. Even so, she realized she had never felt like she was as much of a part of the community as she was now. Everyone seemed to know who she was, by her talent if not her face, and she knew she would need to do some extra baking the next few weeks to keep up with the additional orders that would undoubtedly come rolling in. The mayor said he would talk to his wife about coming in to order a cake like the one on raffle, and several businesswomen had asked for her card. Just Like Grandma's was going to be flooded with requests for Christmas goodies.

"I can't believe this," Sammy mused to her boss as yet more people came crowding in the door and the waiters brought an additional table out of the back. "I guess the Radical Grandmas aren't the only ones who want to save the rec center."

Towards the end of the evening Helen absently said

"Mmhmm." Her neck was straight and her eyes squinted as she looked across the room.

"What is it?" Sammy had only seen a friendly smile and a

relaxed warmth on Helen's face up until this point, but now she looked downright angry.

"Do you see that woman over there by the dessert table? The brunette with her hair in a bun and a green dress?"

Sammy spotted the woman in question easily. She was bending down to examine each pudding individually, her head tipping from side to side. At one point, she even picked up a platter and gave one of the puddings a good sniff. "I can't tell if she's excited about the puddings or repulsed by them. I know it's not a traditional thing around here, so I'm not sure how well they'll go over. They'll either ruin my baking business or boost the numbers through the roof. Maybe I should go give her my card."

Helen put a staying hand on Sammy's wrist. "That woman is Carly Anderson, and she owns Carly's Cupcakes."

"Oh." Sammy had seen the brightly colored sign for the bakery on the other end of town, but she hadn't thought about it much. She could sense the suspicion in Helen's voice. "What do you think she's doing?"

Her boss leaned close so that nobody would overhear. "Rumor has it that her bakery isn't doing so hot. Of course, you're selling out every day, so Carly probably feels like she's in serious competition with you. She might be sabotaging the puddings."

"Surely not!" Sammy was inclined to think the best about

people, even those who were in the same market as she was. "Wouldn't that be a bit obvious?"

Helen shrugged. "There are a lot of people here, and they're probably not paying that much attention to her. I'd like to think she's just interested, but you never know."

Sammy fiddled with the silver bracelet she had put on for the occasion, trying to decide what to do. She could introduce herself and pretend as though nothing untoward was happening. Simply being near the puddings would probably drive Carly away if she had any bad intentions, and if not then she would have met someone new. But what if Carly didn't want to play nice? The last thing Sammy wanted was to create a scene at this fundraiser, since she knew just how important it was to the Grandmas.

But someone else was making a scene for her. Jamie Stewart came running in the door that led out to the pool, letting it slam shut behind her. She was screaming something unintelligible, clutching her fingers in her curly brown hair. The wait staff stopped and stared, and most of the guests did so as well. It wasn't until the band stopped playing that Sammy could finally understand what she was saying. "There's a dead body in the pool!"

Jamie had been in every play throughout junior high and high school, always snagging the lead role. She had a flare for the dramatic, and Sammy was inclined to think this was just some sort of elaborate prank. But as guests began gathering at the glass door to the pool and someone else started screaming, Sammy knew this was for real. Her curiosity overwhelmed her, and she joined the crowd at the long line of windows on that side of the room.

The overhead lights in the pool room had been left off for the occasion, leaving the rows of lounge chairs around the outer edge in shadows. But the underwater lights—several of which had gone out—illuminated the warm water of the pool. This made the silhouette of the body in the pool show up in stark relief, but there was no mistaking the red satin dress or the sensible shoes. It was Maureen Bradshaw.

4

GOODWILL TOWARD MEN

S ammy walked slowly back to her seat, her heart in her stomach. "It's Maureen," she whispered to Helen as she sank into her chair, unable to believe what she had just seen and wishing she hadn't looked at all. "Maybe we should go."

"All right, everyone. Keep it calm, please." Sheriff Jones appeared seemingly out of nowhere. He had likely been there the entire time, but Sammy had been busy enough meeting new people that she hadn't noticed him. Dressed in uniform, he spoke quickly and quietly into his radio.

"I think we'd better stay, at least for the moment," Helen advised. "I don't think they really like it when people leave in these situations."

Sammy couldn't argue with that, but it was incredibly uncomfortable to watch as the paramedics, two detectives, and several more police officers filed into the building a few minutes later and headed out to the pool. The overhead lights were turned on, but Sammy kept her gaze on her plate of half-eaten food. "I just can't believe this. What do you think happened?"

"I wouldn't even want to speculate," Helen replied softly. "But she wasn't young, and we know she was stressed this afternoon. Maybe she had a heart attack."

It was a reasonable conclusion, and one that Sammy could take some small comfort in. If so, then Maureen died doing what she loved. It was still a shame, though. Maureen had been such a lively woman.

Just then, the sheriff came back into the dining area. "I need to talk to someone who knew Mrs. Bradshaw well. I need to know what she might have been allergic to."

Agnes stepped forward timidly, her fingers shaking near her mouth. "Just nuts, officer."

"There were nuts in the puddings!" someone shouted from the back of the crowd. "And I saw her eating one!"

"There were not!" Sammy was on her feet in an instant, hardly even realizing she had said the words. She didn't know who had claimed there were nuts in the puddings, but it didn't matter because she knew the truth. The crowd turned as one to look at her, and she felt their gaze just as much as she saw it. She cleared her throat. "I made those myself, and she specifically requested that there be no nuts."

Sheriff Jones' blue eyes were heavy on her then. He spotted her across the room and shook his head. "I'll need you to stay put for a while, Ms. Baker."

Sammy nodded and sat, knowing exactly what the sheriff was thinking. She had been nothing but trouble for him ever since she had come back to Sunny Cove, and tonight wasn't going to be any different. She sat back down, knowing that she would be questioned about the incident once the police got the scene cleared out a little. "There really weren't any nuts," Sammy muttered to Helen. "Almost all the recipes called for them, but I definitely left them out. Some even suggested using ground almonds in place of bread crumbs, and I didn't do that either. You can check the dumpster for wrappers."

Helen's cool hand stroked her arm. "I know, dear, I know. Don't you worry about a thing."

The police were taking down the names of everyone at the party, slowly dismissing them by table. Sammy watched them go, wishing she was one of them. "I'd hate to spend Christmas in jail, especially for something I didn't do. My father had to spend plenty of holidays that way before they finally set him free." The news about Maureen had been terrible enough, but it made Sammy sad all over again to think of her father. If he was still alive, maybe the two of them would have been able to spend the holidays together. But she was as alone as she had always been. At least she would have church on Christmas morning, as long as Alfred Jones didn't insist

CHRISTMAS PUDS & KILLERS

that she spend it with him in the county jail. She bowed her head and sent up a prayer that true justice would be served.

She was disturbed by the sound of a chair being pulled out next to her. It was Linda. "Honey, don't look so glum," she consoled, her diamond drop earrings glittering. "We know you didn't do anything wrong."

"And we're the closest thing Maureen has—had—to family around here." This was Viola, who now sat across from Sammy. "We can stop the police from pursuing this if it becomes an issue."

Agnes filled up the last empty chair. "I'm sure they'll have some other tests to do, but I heard one of the paramedics say her throat was swollen. Maybe there's something else she was allergic to that we don't know about."

"Or there were nuts in something else, something that came with the dinner, perhaps," Viola pointed out. "Either way, don't you worry Sammy. We're going to help."

She was so moved she wanted to cry, and as a tear slipped down her cheek she realized she couldn't help it. "That's very sweet of you ladies, but you have a friend to mourn. I'm sure you don't want to get involved in this."

"We do, actually." Linda set her hands on the table, her rings clinking against it. "We know you didn't kill Maureen. You're not that kind of person, and if you were we never would have asked for your help. But we need to figure out what happened to our friend, and if clearing your name helps us with that, then I can't think of a better way to spend our time."

Sammy picked up her napkin and dabbed at her eye. "But how are you going to do that? None of us are detectives, unless one of you has a hidden talent you didn't tell me about."

Agnes held her head proudly in the air, tears still glistening in her bright eyes. "Maybe not, but I can tell you that I've watched every episode of *Murder, She Wrote* and *Columbo*."

"That was over twenty years ago," Linda pointed out.

"That's true, but my grandson got me all set up with that streaming television service over the summer. It has all that on there and more. That new Sherlock is good, but I don't think I have quite his talents."

Even so, the idea seemed to be catching on. Sammy spotted a gleam in Viola's eye. "I have quite a bit of experience myself, if you want to count all the mysteries I read in my spare time at the library. If you pick up any book by Rita Mae Brown or Lillian Jackson Braun, I can promise you I will have read it."

"Those are just cozy mysteries," Linda argued.

"But people die in them, and the killers are found," Viola pointed out. "I've also read plenty of Agatha Christie, Mary Higgins Clark, and probably anyone else you can think of. You can learn anything when you pick up a book, even if it's fiction."

Linda looked as though she wanted to argue with this for a moment, but then she raised an eyebrow toward Sammy. "You know, if you need someone to crunch some numbers, I used to be an accountant."

Sammy smiled at them all. They were such wonderful ladies, and even in the face of tragedy they were thinking about what needed to be done next. "I hope it doesn't come down to that."

"Doesn't matter either way. We're all a team now, and we're going to get this figured out. You're in too, right Helen?"

The restaurant owner was only a few years younger than the Grandmas, and Sammy thought she looked like she would fit right in with them. The biggest difference was that she insisted on continuing to work. "You bet."

"Great! I know things are crazy right now, and we're all going to need at least a little time to grieve. Us Grandmas have already seen plenty in our lifetimes, so we should be ready to go by tomorrow. How about we get together tomorrow afternoon to get started?" Linda slapped the table with authority.

"Make it a little later in the day and we can meet at the diner after it's closed," Helen offered.

Sammy smiled through her tears. "I'll serve up all the cake and goodies you gals can eat."

The women all nodded their heads and agreed, discussing what time would be best for everyone. Sammy hadn't known the Grandmas for very long, but already she felt as though she was an honorary part of their group. They didn't have to stick up for her or help her out with this, but she knew they would even if she tried to say no.

Sheriff Jones interrupted their conversation as he stepped up to the table, his thumbs tucked into his belt. "If you ladies would excuse us, I need to speak to Ms. Baker for a moment."

Sammy stood slowly, her legs shaking underneath her. She had talked with Sheriff Jones several times before, but it was still intimidating when she knew she might be a suspect. She forced a smile at the other ladies. "Why don't you go on home and get some rest? It's already so late."

"Are you sure?" Agnes asked, giving a piercing stare to Sheriff Jones. "We can stick around."

"It'll be fine, really," he assured them. If Jones was interested in putting her in handcuffs, he probably would have already done it.

"I'll see you tomorrow," Sammy quietly said.

The interview with Sheriff Jones was fairly routine, and he seemed to believe her when she told him she had left nuts out of each and every one of the puddings. Still, she had already been exhausted, and the effort of going over all the details drained the rest of her remaining energy. He let her go but remained behind to talk to some of the kitchen staff.

On the spur of the moment, Sammy exited through the pool room. It might not have been the right thing to do, but she felt that if she stood there for a moment and watched the brightly lit water lap at the sides of the pool she might be able to pay a small homage to the strong, spritely woman who had been a part of her life for such a short time.

Yellow police tape stretched from one wall to the other across the room and over the top of the pool, segmenting it off from the concrete walkway that led to the exit. Large, wet boot prints led away from the scene on the other side of the pool, slowly drying as the water absorbed into the concrete. Sammy knew this was not how Maureen would want her precious rec center to be remembered, and she could only hope that the fundraiser would be enough. As she stood there, inhaling the thick scent of chlorine, she imagined what it must have been like that fateful day when the four women met during water aerobics classes. In her mind's eye, she could see them slowly start talking to one another, building their bonds over underwater arm curls and kicks. It must have been a beautiful, magical thing for the four of them, and now at least part of it was over.

Just as she turned to leave, something floating in the

water caught Sammy's eye. She turned back to see a scrap of paper bumping up against the side of the pool, the small waves created by the filter forcing it into a corner. Sammy glanced around. Nobody was watching. On an instinct that she couldn't resist, she swiped it out of the water and headed for her car.

5

MAKE A LIST

"**I** hope the sheriff wasn't too hard on you," Agnes fussed, her thin eyebrows knitting together. "He didn't look very pleased when he left last night."

"That's the way Alfie looks anytime he's on the case," Helen explained as she pulled a stack of dessert plates out. "But he's never as mean as he looks."

"Alfie?" Linda questioned.

"He grew up across the street from my house," Helen said with a smile. "Of course, he wants everyone to call him Sheriff now, but I just can't. He's always going to be Alfie to me."

"Well, good. Then maybe we can use your connection to him if we need to."

Sammy smiled as she brought out a layer cake she had made with the leftover batter and frosting from her creation for the fundraiser. She had been concerned about how this meeting would go, simply because she didn't think there was much the five of them could do to figure out Maureen's death. But as they all sat down and chatted like old friends, she knew it would be all right. They might not be professional detectives, but they could at least have a good time while they tried.

"Oh, Sammy! This is gorgeous!" Viola gushed as she turned her plate around to look at her piece of cake from all angles.

"It's just a vanilla layer cake, nothing special." It had seemed like a shame to waste the extra batter, and her initial idea had been to put it up for sale with her other baked goods. But it was the perfect size for them to share, and it seemed a fitting tribute to Maureen.

"Nothing special, my foot! You put Carly's Cupcakes to shame." She swallowed her cake and tapped the end of her fork on the table. "Now, how do we need to go about this? I understand you've solved a mystery or two lately, Ms. Baker."

Sammy lifted one shoulder and let it fall. "I just got lucky, that's all. But I do think we should discuss who might be interested in killing Maureen. We need to find someone who had the right motivation to do such a horrible thing. Did she have any enemies?" She had brought a notebook and a pen with her to the meeting, and she sat poised to write. Notes always seemed to help when she was trying to figure something out.

Linda ran her fingers back and forth over the large pearls

of her necklace as she thought. "I can't really think of anyone. I mean, Maureen wasn't particularly *liked* by a lot of people, but I don't think they would have killed her over it."

"Why didn't they like her?" Sammy was intrigued.

"She simply wasn't the type of woman who sat down and shut up. Maureen always stood up for what she believed in, and she never accepted excuses. She would never bend morals for the sake of profit or fun or popularity." Agnes smiled at remembering her friend. "She was as hard as they come."

"Oh, and she loved to argue," Viola added. "There wasn't a topic she didn't know how to debate. If she wanted to save a tree from getting cut down in the park, then she could find a reason to keep it from happening. Maureen always came out on top."

"More recently was that land developer...what's his name?" Linda paused with a forkful of cake in the air as she tried to remember.

"Andrew Herzog," Viola answered instantly as she scraped the last of the icing from her plate.

"A land developer?" Sammy questioned, writing down the man's name. She had heard the name, but she couldn't imagine what a man like that would have to do with Maureen.

"It's been a whole big thing over the last several months," Viola expounded. "It all started because of the rec center, you see. Herzog's goal is to build houses, hotels, and office complexes all over this city, and he doesn't care what he knocks out of the way to do it. The rec center just happened to be on his list of buildings."

"Maureen wouldn't stand for it," Agnes volunteered. "She was the one handling that end of things, so I don't know all the details, but I do know that he wanted to build some high-rise condo on that spot."

"But do you really think a business deal is worth killing over?" Helen mused. She had taken the smallest piece of cake, citing that she was trying to watch her figure, but now she cut herself a second one. "And I wouldn't think Maureen would even be the one in charge of making that decision."

"That never mattered to Maureen," Linda advised. "She didn't require an official capacity to state her opinion or how she felt about the issue. As a matter of fact, she and Mr. Herzog were arguing about it last night, right after the fundraiser had started."

Sammy was writing as quickly as she could now. "They did? What did they say?"

"I didn't catch the whole thing. I had just come back from fetching some eggnog for myself when I saw him talking to her. Even when I wasn't within earshot, I could tell that things weren't going well. I came up just in time to hear him say that old buildings needed to be moved out of the way, and so did cranky old women like Maureen!"

"That certainly sounds suspicious," Helen agreed, nodding her head.

"Did she tell you any details?" Sammy asked.

Linda sighed. "No, I'm afraid she didn't. And I didn't push her, because I knew she would just want to get the event underway and move past anything negative. Come to think of it, I don't even know why Mr. Herzog would have been at the party, anyway, not if he wanted the place torn down."

"It's definitely a start." Sammy flipped to a clean sheet of paper, since she had already filled the first one. "Anything else? Anyone else who might have been after her?"

The ladies sat back against the cushioned booth, thinking. "I really don't know of anyone," Agnes said. "As I said, most people didn't like her, but it wasn't anything worth murder."

"Fair enough. Maybe we can talk about what she had done over the last few days. There could be a clue there." She was grasping at straws now, but they couldn't just leave it at one suspect and call it a closed case.

"I know she went to the doctor a few days ago," Viola offered, "but that was just a routine checkup. I know because I drove her. The doctor said she was healthy as a horse and stubborn as a mule."

"She went to a church meeting," Agnes said, eyeing the rest of the cake. "She was relatively quiet, only arguing with the pastor and a few of the deacons about little things. Nothing unusual."

Linda adjusted her earrings. "She told me that she took her granddaughter Christmas shopping over at Gibb's Department Store. Last year she went over to the big mall in Oak Hills and stayed at that fancy hotel while her daughter's house was getting remodeled, but there was that big burglary by an insider at the hotel. That put the kibosh on her holiday traveling for sure."

"Speaking of Gibb's, did you see how terrible the store Santa is this year?" Viola asked, her tongue sharpening. "He doesn't seem to care about the children at all. I took my grandson there last weekend, hoping they had the same sweet old man that has been there in the past, but this one didn't seem to care at all about what Johnny wanted for Christmas."

"You know, you're not the only one to complain." Agnes was a sweet and almost ditzy lady, but she suddenly looked angry. "I've heard people all over town talking about how terrible he is, that he doesn't do the whole routine of asking if they've been good boys and girls and what would they like and that they have to make sure they go to bed on Christmas Eve. He just pastes on a smile for the picture and waves the kid on."

"I think Mr. McLaughlin must have gotten some sort of bargain basement Santa this year," Linda affirmed. "It's a shame that the stores care more about how much profit they make than doing something good for the community. I know Gibb's is a store, not a charity or a church, but our experiences there still mean a lot to us. I remember taking my own children there to sit on Santa's lap. It was something we always looked forward to, and I was sad when it was over."

"If you think the Santa is a shame, then have you seen the 'specials' they've brought in?" Viola scoffed. "The place is full to the brim with extra clothes, and they're priced so well that I could probably outfit my entire family even on my retiree's budget, but I don't think they would last past the first wash."

Sammy cleared her throat. "As interesting as all this is, I don't think it's going to help us figure out what happened to Maureen," she said gently. She had taken note of the places the women had mentioned, even though there didn't seem to be anything odd about them. "Maybe we could do what the police did and make a list of everyone who was there, especially anyone who might have been acting a little strange."

"Why don't you just go to Jones and ask? He seems to like you," Helen suggested.

The other women hooted and rubbed shoulders like a bunch of teenagers.

Sammy's face flushed. "I don't think there's anything like that going on. From the way he looks at me, he would just as soon I go running back to New York than to stay here and cause trouble for him. Besides, he would never give me that sort of information. I'm sure it's police business."

"Well, since you mentioned it, what about Carly Anderson?" Helen asked.

Linda raised an eyebrow. "From Carly's Cupcakes?"

"That's the one," Helen affirmed. "She was lurking around those Christmas puddings like a vulture. Maybe she was jealous that you were the one asked to provide the desserts for this shindig, and it was no secret that Maureen was allergic to nuts. She could have slipped one in."

"I don't know," Sammy said, although she made a note of the name. "There would be no guarantee that Maureen would eat it, and that seems like a pretty extreme way to go about framing me just to get me out of the way." She also really didn't like the idea that Maureen could have gotten caught up in something that was about her. That was the most uncomfortable thought of all.

"But think about it," Helen advised. "You were already accused of poisoning someone with your baked goods before, when the sheriff got sick. You and your reputation recovered from that pretty well, but I can see how it could have given Carly an idea or two."

"I'll keep it in mind, but I think we'll leave it as a last resort if nothing else comes up."

"So what do we do now?" Agnes asked, clapping her hands together and looking at the group. "Hit the streets and search for clues?"

"In a way, I guess so," Sammy agreed. "Can you ladies

contact those who she knew best? Friends, family, people she knew from church, and see if they know anything? They'll be more willing to talk to you than anyone else."

The Grandmas nodded their agreement.

"Great. I guess I'll talk to the land developer and see what I can find out. I'll have to come up with some excuse to go there."

Helen gestured at the diner around them. "Why not ask him about building a new place for Just Like Grandma's? It's the sort of thing he'll be interested in, considering this place has been here for about a hundred years. There's nothing really wrong with it that a little bit of regular maintenance doesn't take care of, but he'll only be thinking about the money."

Viola tapped her finger on the table. "I can talk with her neighbors, see if they saw anything suspicious."

"Sounds like we've got it all covered," Sammy said with a smile. "Let's see what we can find out."

6

CHECK IT TWICE

Sammy had the next day off. It was good timing, since that allowed her to explore the circumstances of Maureen's death without having to interfere with her work time, but it also didn't give her much headway in making appointments and planning her day. Fortunately, it had taken only a simple phone call to get in with Andrew Herzog.

"Oh, you look lovely!" Helen enthused as Sammy came down the stairs from her apartment and into the kitchen. "I don't think I've ever seen you look so dressed up." Johnny gave her a thumbs-up from over by the griddle.

Smoothing down the dark blue skirt suit and wishing she had some more comfortable shoes to match it, Sammy felt her cheeks flush a little. "I thought I should look professional if I'm going to pretend to be interested in spending a bunch of money with this man. He might not believe me if I show up in an apron covered with flour."

"You'll fool him just fine!" Helen said with a grin. "The next thing I know you'll become a master of disguise and I won't even recognize you when you have a mystery to solve!"

Sammy adjusted her purse on her shoulder and jingled her keys in her hand, a nervous knot taking up residence in her stomach. "Helen, do you think this whole idea is ridiculous?"

"What, talking to Mr. Herzog?"

"No, more of trying to figure out what happened to Maureen. I feel like I'm too old to be playing Nancy Drew, running around spying on people and trying to get information out of them. I don't know anything about detective work, and we don't even know that there's a *reason* to investigate. The police haven't said."

Helen placed a gentle hand on each of her arms. "Sammy, my dear, I could never say that it's ridiculous. You are always busy with something, and I find that admirable. So many people are content to lay around watching television or playing on their phones without a care for what's going on in the world, but you aren't like that. And don't ever say you're too old. The Radical Grandmas are twice your age at least, and wasn't Miss Marple up there in years?"

Sammy laughed. "I thought Viola was the mystery novel expert."

"I've read a book or two in my day," Helen said with a smile. "And you should know better than to think there's nothing going on simply because the police haven't said anything. Alfie Jones is a good man and a smart one, and I trust him to do his job, but part of doing his job means not releasing any information to the public until the time is right. He can't just come out and say Maureen was murdered unless he has good cause, and he won't want to drive Sunny Cove into a panic. Especially not around the holidays."

"You're always the voice of reason, aren't you?" Sammy asked, feeling comfort in knowing that she could count on someone so close to her. The two women spent a lot of time together, and that would be difficult if they didn't have such a good relationship.

"I try! Now, you get out there and find us a new pretend restaurant!"

As she drove across town, Sammy felt a little guilty at the idea that she had to deceive Mr. Herzog in order to get information out of him. It didn't seem fair to make him think he would be initiating a new business deal, when she knew good and well it would never happen. "Lord, I know you understand why I'm doing this," she whispered, tightening her grip on the steering wheel. I just hope you can forgive me for it."

Mr. Herzog's office was a large and flashy one, two levels of dark concrete lines with so many windows that they reflected the buildings across the street. If this was a larger city, Sammy was certain he would have built a skyscraper instead. Her stomach flopped around as she walked across the parking lot and entered the massive lobby, complete with a metal modern art sculpture hanging from the ceiling. A sophisticated-looking young woman sat behind a desk in the back of the lobby, and she looked up as soon as Sammy walked in.

"Ms. Baker?"

How did she know? "Yes, ma'am. I'm here to see Mr. Herzog."

But of course the secretary already knew that. "Right this way, please." She led Sammy down a curving hallway past a series of office doors, and Sammy had to wonder just how many people this man had working for him. The secretary opened the largest door at the end of the hall and waved her into a massive office. "Please, have a seat. Mr. Herzog will be with you momentarily. Would you like a bottle of water or some coffee?"

"No, thank you," she replied nervously as she sank into the metal chair in front of a large glass desk. This was all too much for a small place like Sunny Cove. If Herzog wanted to transform the town into a big city, then he had certainly started with his own office.

After less than a minute, a door behind the desk opened and a very tall man walked in. Sammy craned her head back to see his face at such close proximity. He was slim in his brown tailored suit, and he gave her a cold smile as he reached out to shake her hand. His other hand was tucked around a thin laptop. "Ms. Baker, thank you for being so prompt. I know we have a lot to discuss."

Her misgivings about lying to him swelled within her once again, but she reminded herself that it was for Maureen's sake. And perhaps she would need her own building in the future if she decided to open her own bakery, although the idea of leaving Helen seemed impossible. "Yes. We're interested in seeing what you might be able to do for us in terms of a new restaurant."

Andrew sat down, but he was still a good head taller than Sammy. Still it made it easier to speak to him without focusing on his height. He opened his laptop, which was more like a fancy tablet with a keyboard attached, and nodded. "Your current location is 1214 Main Street, is that correct?"

"Yes, sir." Sammy didn't know why he intimidated her so much. Maybe it was because she knew he was the prime suspect in Maureen's death, or maybe because he was such a prominent business man who clearly had a lot of money to throw around. She reminded herself that she was important, too. Doughnuts, rolls, and muffins might not be as important as new buildings, but people certainly seemed to want them.

"Yes, I thought so. I took the liberty of pulling up the city plans for the place. It was built in the 1930s, and I'm sure I don't have to tell you that building codes were much different back then. It's remarkable the place is still standing." He scrolled through his notes on the screen.

"Well, it's had several remodels. The second floor is actually a very nice apartment."

"But certainly a small one," he countered, shaking his head. "It's not really enough living space to be considered decent, and the idea of having living quarters over a place of business is incredibly old-fashioned. You need something new and modern, something that will catch people's eye and make them realize how much they want to explore the new and different."

Sammy opened her mouth to protest that she very much liked her small apartment, thank you very much, and it was more than enough for a single person who wasn't home all that often anyway. But she snapped it shut again, reminding herself that she wasn't here to defend their building and what it meant to them. "Yes, that's exactly right."

"And the name?" Andrew raised a light brown eyebrow that matched his short crew cut. "Just Like Grandma's? That really isn't going to bring in a crowd. I know you're here for a new building, but I know a great marketing guy that I can set you up with. He can completely revamp the place, from the name to the furniture to the menus. And you're going to want it once you get into a new building. Your old stuff simply won't look right."

"I'm sure that's true. But for now, I think I'd just like to start with the building. I'll need that information to take back to my business partner and see what she thinks." Change the name? Redo the menus? Did this man never go out and interact with any of the people in Sunny Cove?

Customers young and old flocked to Just Like Grandma's on a regular basis. It probably had nothing to do with the name of the diner and more to do with the fact that they could get a good meal for a cheap price, and they always knew they would get great service.

"And I've got something that's going to knock her socks off." Andrew turned the tablet around, displaying a behemoth of brick and glass with odd little pergolas sticking out every now and then. Everything was angles and corners and lighting. "Here's the exterior, which is going to reach out and grab anyone who drives by. I've got the floor plan here as well."

"It's...so big." She couldn't think of anything else nice to say about it. It would hold half the town. While that might seem like a good thing to a man like Andrew Herzog, Sammy knew it would completely take away the cozy, small-town feeling that came from their current place. They would have to hire five times their current staff, at least. And it was far too modern for a diner that served biscuits and gravy and homestyle stew.

"Exactly! People don't like to feel crowded. They want to spread out a little, make themselves at home. The key is to have free Wi-Fi and outlets at every table. The internet is everywhere, and you don't want your restaurant to be the exception." The enthusiasm was obvious on the developer's face.

But Sammy wasn't so sure that it was a bad thing to be the exception. People sat down with their families and actually

CHRISTMAS PUDS & KILLERS

talked to each other while they ate. Sure, they still checked their phones, but it would be awful for Just Like Grandma's to turn into an internet café with nothing but the sound of clacking keyboards and coffee machines. "It's always good to stay on top of current trends," she said nervously.

"I'll email you a copy of everything so you can go over it with your partner. It also includes a bid sheet from the contractor."

Sammy nodded, knowing Helen would laugh so hard she would fall out of her chair once she saw it. "I guess my biggest question for you right now is where such a place would be built? It's much bigger than the footprint of our current place."

Andrew waved off the idea of their Main Street location. "I've got the perfect place. There's a place near the edge of town, right next to the new gas station."

"The only place I can think of is the Dairy Queen."

"Exactly! That place is ancient, and it needs to be razed so something new can grow there. I've got the owners just about ready to sell."

This was about as much as Sammy could tolerate. She certainly knew a lot more about this man's characters after spending only a few minutes with him, and it was time to get to the heart of the matter. Snapping her fingers in the air, she said, "That's what it is! I've been trying to figure out where I've seen you before. You were at the fundraiser the other night for the Sunny Cove Recreation Center, weren't you?"

"Ugh, unfortunately." Mr. Herzog's bright, positive disposition took an instant downturn. "What a miserable old place! I can't believe anyone would want to save it. And while I know it's not right to speak of the dead, it will never get registered with the historical society now that Maureen is gone."

"Oh." Sammy wasn't sure how well she was hiding her shock at this revelation. "I didn't realize that it qualified to be on the register."

Andrew rolled his eyes. "Yeah, some bunk about it having a lasting effect on the community and the important people in our past who went there, yada yada yada. It's just a rundown swimming pool, and there's no reason to keep dumping money into it when I could build a high-rise condo that would really have an impact." He turned the computer around, pulled up a different file, and showed it to her. "Look at this place. It's gorgeous, and it would house so many people in Sunny Cove who are currently living in old, dilapidated bungalows. Not to mention the employees that would be involved as well."

The monstrosity on the screen was again all angles and glass, and the height of it would make it stick out like a sore thumb in their tiny town. "I see. And you think you'll be able to build that now?"

"Not a problem," he assured her. "It's time it was moved out of the way for the sake of progress. If it weren't for men like me, Sunny Cove would still be just a collection of stick shacks without so much as a general store."

"I'm sure you're right. I think I have everything I need for the moment. I'll be sure to get back to you." Sammy scurried out of the office as quickly as she could without giving herself away. It had certainly been an interesting interview.

7

HOLIDAY BAKING

B ack in her car, heading through the damp slush that the snow plow had left behind, Sammy took a deep breath and sighed. Mr. Herzog was definitely determined to get rid of the rec center, but was he determined enough to kill Maureen? She seemed to be the only force standing in his way, and he was certainly interested in knocking down the old to bring in the new, but Sammy hadn't really found out anything conclusive. It was time to move on and explore something else for a while.

Unfortunately, she knew just where she needed to go, and she wasn't looking forward to it. Helen's insistence that Carly Anderson was involved somehow was a thought that had nagged at the back of Sammy's mind all night, and the only way to feel better about it was go talk to her. But Sammy wasn't interested in creating an enemy out of this woman—that is, if Carly didn't already see her as an enemy—and she wasn't as confident that her cover story would work. Why would a baker visit another baker's shop, after all?

But as she pulled up in front of Carly's Cupcakes, she knew she had to try. It would settle her mind, and it would be another person to cross off the list. She desperately wanted to show the Radical Grandmas that she was all on board with this case, and this little visit would prove it to herself as well.

The scent of sugar and butter was thick in the air as soon as she got out of her car. The old building had been painted a muted shade of hunter green, but the brilliant pink and white awning and the decorative painting on the front window made it obvious what sort of place this was. "Carly's Cupcakes" stood out in bold, swirling pink letters above a display of her goods in a glass case. Sammy's throat was tight as she walked in, hoping there would be plenty of other customers in front of her so she would have a chance to look around the place before she had to talk to anyone.

But she wasn't going to be that lucky. The place was completely empty. The black and white checkerboard tile was swept clean around a few small tables along one side of the store near a refrigerated case of cold drinks. The big glass cases that filled up two other walls displayed a variety of cupcakes, cookies, and muffins. The pink theme carried over on the interior, with the drywall behind the cases painted a bright pink trimmed in white. No employees were in sight.

With shaking fingers, Sammy stepped forward and rang

the little silver bell on the counter. She eyed the Christmas-themed cupcakes in the case in front of her, each with a tiny candy cane perched on top, ready to order half a dozen of them if things were too awkward.

A woman emerged from the back, dusting her fingers off on her apron. Sammy immediately recognized her dark hair—once again pulled up in a bun—and her long, sharp face. Carly smiled toward her latest customer, but the smile faded and her skin turned pale as soon as she saw Sammy. "Oh. Um, hello."

It wasn't the friendliest greeting, but Sammy knew she wasn't the type of customer Carly had been expecting. She remembered to smile. "Hi! I'm Sammy Baker. I work down at Just Like Grandma's." She held out her hand, hoping she looked more confident than she felt.

"Yes, I've heard all about you," Carly replied as she slowly reached out to shake her hand. "And I've heard how talented you are. Is there something I can help you with?"

"Maybe, if you have a minute to talk."

Carly gestured around them at the empty bakery. "I don't have anyone else occupying my time right now."

Sammy pulled in a deep breath, hoping her idea didn't come back to kick her in the behind later. "Sometimes we're asked to do catering jobs or special orders for birthdays and parties. This really seems to pick up around the holidays, and sometimes it's more than we can keep up with. I thought I would check with you to see if I could refer some of the work to you." It had been the most flattering and least contentious pretext Sammy had been able to come up with, and it was something that might actually work out to both of their advantages.

Carly's attitude completely changed, and a slow and excited smile spread over her face. "Why don't you have a seat, and we can chat?" She pointed at the tables on the opposite side of the room.

Now they were getting somewhere. "Sure."

The baker brought two cupcakes to the table with her, placing one in front of Sammy. They were the cute Christmas ones with the mini candy canes. "Cup of coffee?"

"That would be great." There was nothing better on a cold, snowy day than a hot cup of coffee. Once they were both settled in, Sammy peeled back the wrapper on her cupcake. "I appreciate you taking time out of your day to talk with me. I wasn't sure how you would feel about me, since apparently some people see us as competition. Personally, I don't think of it that way."

Carly looked relieved. "I'm glad to hear that, and that you're willing to send a little business my way. I opened this shop on a bit of a whim, and things have been pretty slow."

"Have you done any sort of advertising?" Just Like Grandma's didn't dive into their marketing any further than posting their specials in the front window, but the diner had been around for so long and had so many regulars that they didn't need much more than word of mouth. A new business was different, she was sure.

"I've tried, but I haven't had much luck. I think there are a lot of people who are baking at home these days, watching cooking shows and just deciding they want to do it on their own. And maybe my prices are a little high, but ingredients are expensive!" Carly plucked the candy cane off the top of her cupcake and set it aside on a napkin.

"I can't argue with you there. I do a lot of volume, but our profit margin on the baked goods probably isn't as high as people think. And then of course, there's all the time I invest in it as well." The first bite of her cupcake had been pretty good, with a nice minty flavor in the cake balanced out by the creaminess of the icing. But as she bit into the center, she found that the cake had suddenly turned dense and overly moist. It had fallen in the middle, and while this had been covered up with the icing for appearances, it didn't make for the most appealing treat. "I think you're overmixing your batter."

As she said it, she looked up to see the pure horror on Carly's face. Sammy hadn't meant to say anything critical; it was just an automatic response. She had just started up her conversation with this woman and hadn't even gotten close to talking about the party, and she had already ruined it. "I'm so sorry. I didn't mean anything by it."

"No. No, it's all right. I've been wondering how to fix that." She stared at her own cupcake for a moment before jumping up from the table. At first, Sammy thought Carly would attack her or at least kick her out, but she trotted around behind the display case. "Here. Try this one. I wanted to make a lemon cupcake. My grandma used to bake them when I was a little kid, but I never could find her recipe. I found another recipe and I follow it to the tee every time, but they always come out tasting funny."

Sammy gamely tried the bright yellow cupcake and immediately knew what the problem was. The confection tasted more like sugary floor cleaner than a lemon cupcake. "Are you using artificial flavoring?"

"I got a really good deal on it online," Carly explained, looking sheepish.

Sammy couldn't even pretend to finish this one, and she set it back down in its wrapper. "I understand, but lemons aren't all that pricey. A little bit of zest and juice from the real thing instead of the artificial stuff will really go a long way."

"Thank you! I'll be sure to try that!" Carly picked up the cake in question and put it in the trash. "I like to think I at least have decent coffee, right?"

Sammy took a sip, happy to find that the owner was right. "That, I can't argue with."

"I'm so embarrassed. I always loved to bake as a kid. It was my dream to open up a place like this for the longest time. I had it all planned out with a binder full of recipes and paint swatches and ideas. And when my grandma died and left me an inheritance, I thought it was the perfect chance to finally live out my fantasy. My family was really excited for me, too, but sometimes I wonder if I ever should have done this." She hung her head sadly as she sat back down.

"Don't let a few botched recipes get you down," Sammy replied sympathetically, reaching across the table to touch Carly on the arm. "It happens to everyone."

"Maybe you're right. Maybe I just need a little more practice. And I should get out in the community more instead of hiding in the kitchen so people will actually know who I am. That seems to go a long way in Sunny Cove." Carly's eyes were glistening with tears, but the corners of her mouth trembled into a smile.

"That's a great idea!" Sammy couldn't have asked for a better moment to bring up the real reason she had come. "I think I saw you at the fundraiser for the rec center a few days ago, didn't I?"

"Oh. Yeah." Carly's color blanched again slightly, and she began clearing their table. "Quite the party!"

"Did you get a chance to try any of the Christmas puddings? Those were such a challenge! I never thought I could pull it off, and I have to admit there were a couple of them that went straight into the trash and never saw the light of day." It was the truth, but Sammy thought it might also be a good way for Carly to understand that even she messed up sometimes.

"I doubt that. They were very lovely." Carly's mouth was a straight line as she rearranged a few cupcakes in the display case.

"Did you have a good time at the party? The Radical Grandmas really went out of their way to make it a good old-fashioned Christmas. It's just such a shame about Maureen."

"Yes. Terrible." Carly produced a wet rag and began wiping down the already-immaculate counter around the cash register.

Sammy knew she was no longer welcome, but she had yet to figure out why Carly's attitude had changed so much. "Mind if I take a few of your business cards? That will make it easy for me to refer my extra clients to you."

Carly's shoulders sagged a little as she turned around and grabbed a broom, quickly sweeping the floor. She came around the display cases and attached the kickplates before moving whisking away invisible crumbs under the table they had just been sitting at. "Sure. That'd be great."

"Thanks. I'll give you a call sometime. Maybe we can get together and have lunch, baker to baker," Sammy suggested with a smile.

Somehow, Carly had managed to produce a little dirt with her sweeping. She quickly brushed it into a dustpan and dumped it in the trash. "Sure."

"Thanks. It was great meeting you!" Sammy headed outside, the bell over the door jingling happily. But she didn't feel so happy as she got in her car and set Carly's business cards on the passenger seat next to her. They were white and pink and highly decorated, just like her store. There really could be a potential for the two of them to work together once Carly spent a little more time working on her skills. Unfortunately, there was one big thing that was going to stop that, and as much as Sammy wanted to dismiss it as coincidence, she just couldn't: Carly had swept a sprig of holly into her dustpan.

8

CHRISTMAS TRADITIONS

It had been stressful, but Sammy was glad she had gotten her visit with Carly out of the way. Otherwise, she would have continued to dread it. As it was, she had a few notes to bring back with her the next time she got together with the Radical Grandmas. Sammy drove to her next destination, ready to stop thinking about the young baker.

Gibb's Department Store was a big place compared to the other businesses in Sunny Cove. Two stories tall, it took up almost an entire block downtown. The store had been a resident feature in the town for as long as Sammy could remember, and even her father had spoken to her of going there with his mother when he was a child. The windows, always full of the latest products, had been expertly decorated with garland, Christmas trees, and ornaments amidst the bright sweaters and newest electronics. It might not have been Macy's, but it was close enough for the residents of their little town.

Parking had always been an issue, as much of Sunny Cove's downtown area had been built before cars were the norm. The small lot on the west side of the building was already full, as was the one behind the courthouse half a block away. After circling a few times, Sammy found a slot on the street next to a deep puddle and took it, jumping out of her car to keep her feet from getting wet in the melted snow.

A blast of chilly air tugged at the collar of her coat as she trotted into the store. Sammy hadn't been into Gibb's very much since she had returned home, but at this time of year it gave off a festive feeling that even she couldn't ignore. Looking past the cheap sweat suits that the Radical Grandmas had complained about, she found the same old-fashioned display cases, the staff scurrying around in Santa hats, and the scent of pine in the air.

Just to the left, several racks had been cleared away near the stairs to make room for Santa's chair, complete with a heavy-looking toy sack sitting next to it, oversized fake presents, and an elf to take pictures. Santa, who was filled out with padding and stuffing more than his own jolliness, sat impatiently waiting for the child on his lap to stop talking about the toy train he wanted, get his picture and his candy cane, and leave so the next kid could take their turn. His big black boots were an amusing contrast to his skinny legs in the red suit. There was quite a line of children, even for a weekday, each of them craning their necks to see the magical man.

She browsed through the store, keeping her eyes peeled.

Frank McLaughlin had been the store manager even when she had been a teen and had come in shopping for little black backpack purses and chokers with her friends. Though the other employees would be wearing button-down shirts or sweaters with khakis, Mr. McLaughlin would be dressed in a full three-piece suit. At least, he always had been when she had seen him before, and as she rounded a display of silver watches she saw that nothing had changed.

Mr. McLaughlin was making his rounds of the store, watching that his employees smiled as they rang up purchases and making sure they always asked customers if they needed help. He would pause to adjust a fuzzy bathrobe on a mannequin or put a rack of shirts on hangers back in order by size. This was his castle, and he took his job of keeping it in order very seriously. Sammy knew that he was just doing his job, but she couldn't help but feel a little intimidated as she approached.

"Mr. McLaughlin?"

The older man turned his customer service smile to her. Most of his hairline had receded, leaving a few carefully combed wisps in the front, and his jowls had loosened over the years, but he was still the same man she remembered. "Yes? What can I help you with today? We have a lovely selection of home stereo systems if you're looking for that perfect Christmas gift."

"Well, I do need some help, but not with any shopping." While Sammy had been able to come up with some excuses for visiting her last two suspects, she hadn't found any good way of dealing with the department store manager than being direct. She didn't think of him as a suspect so much as a witness, so it was easier to just be honest. "I have a friend who was in here a few days ago, and she was killed the other day. I'm trying to collect some information on her, to help out the investigation." Sammy added this last part to make her bid for help sound a little more legitimate, even though she had no idea what the police were doing, exactly."

Mr. McLaughlin's chin trembled slightly. His squinty eyes darted around the store, presumably to see if there were any other customers in the vicinity who might overhear the morbid conversation when they were supposed to be surrounded by holiday cheer, and then he gave her a small nod. "Come with me." He turned on the heel of his wingtip oxfords and headed briskly toward the back of the store.

Sammy followed him, struggling to keep pace. They threaded their way through the men's section and housewares until they reached a nondescript door in the wall. He led her into the store room, which was bustling with more workers, and then off to the right and through another door. Now they were in a small office, the metal desk covered in papers and several drawers of the filing cabinet open. "I thought it best that we talk in private. I don't want to give any of my customers a reason to think this isn't a happy place to shop. I hope you understand."

"I do, and I appreciate you taking time out of your busy day to talk to me. I could hardly get a parking spot!" She sat down in the plastic chair Mr. McLaughlin indicated as he moved around the desk to sit down himself.

"That's the way I like it! Just like many businesses, our Christmas season keeps us afloat throughout the rest of the year. Sure, we have our Memorial Day and Labor Day sales, and some good clearance seasons, but there's nothing like the holidays!" He allowed a small smile to crease his face before folding his arms on the top of the desk. "Now, I assume you're here to talk about Maureen Bradshaw. She's the only person I know of who's passed away recently."

"I am," Sammy admitted. She hadn't brought her notebook in with her, but she hoped she would have some good information to jot down in it later. "You see, I have reason to believe that her death might not have been an accident. Some friends and I are doing what we can to figure it all out. I understand that she was in your store just a few days before she died, so I was wondering if you happen to remember her being here."

Mr. McLaughlin shook his head and sighed. "I certainly do remember her being in here, because she was nothing but trouble!"

This wasn't what Sammy had been expecting. "How so?"

Another sigh from the manager. "She was in here with her granddaughter, and I might not have even know she was here amongst the rest of the crowd. But she started making a stink about the clothes I brought in for the holidays. I guess she had checked the tags and realized they were made overseas. She started talking to the other customers about it, and the next thing you know half the store is involved. One of the cashiers came to get me, and I had a hard time convincing her to calm down and that I would handle it."

"I don't think I understand. Lots of clothes are made overseas."

"That's true, but she said this particular company uses a sweatshop. Some Christian group she's associated with has been trying to shut places like this down, and part of that process is creating boycotts against their products. Maureen had checked the tags, and she didn't think it was enough simply not to buy the clothes." Mr. McLaughlin picked up a stack of papers on his desk, tapped them until they were stacked neatly, and set them down again.

"So she was a bit of a problem for you?" Sammy was now second-guessing coming all the way back here alone with this man. If he had anything to do with her death and he now knew that she was onto him, this could be a very dangerous conversation to be having.

"Yes, but I was still very upset to hear that she's gone. Maureen did a lot for this town. She didn't care that her moral authority was going to cut into my profits, but she had good intentions." McLaughlin fiddled with the adjustment knobs on his desk chair.

"Did you notice anything else unusual while she was here? Anyone suspicious or acting oddly?"

The manager shook his head. "Nothing like that at all."

"What about your security guards? Do you think I could speak to them?"

Mr. McLaughlin waved off her request and stood up. "They're busy enough this time of year. Mind you, it's nothing more than a missing sweater here or a shoplifting teen there, but they're very vigilant."

"I understand." What Sammy really understood was that he was done talking to her. "Thanks again for talking with me."

"No problem. Be sure to check out the jewelry counter before you leave. We have some very nice diamond stud earrings in stock."

"Thanks, I'll do that." But Sammy breezed right past the jewelry counter and out the door. She would need to come back later to do some Christmas shopping, but she wasn't in the mood for it at the moment.

When she got back to Just Like Grandma's, she headed straight up the stairs to her apartment and wrote down everything she could remember about her interviews. "I might need to start hiding a digital recorder in my pocket," she muttered as she tapped her pen against her chin and tried to recall all the information.

Stepping over to the sink to make herself some lunch, she caught sight of the soggy piece of paper she had retrieved from the pool at the rec center. Somehow, she had completely forgotten about it until now. At first, it had been so wet that it was impossible to read, and Sammy hadn't been convinced it was recoverable. Now, however, she gently pried it from the clothespin she had hung it from and saw that even though some of the words were blurred, she got the general gist of the article. After a quick lunch, it was time to head to the library.

9

A RIGHT JOLLY OLD ELF

Two days later, Sammy sat at Sheriff Jones' desk at the police station. He sat across from her, tipped back slightly with his muscled arms folded in front of his chest and giving her a somber look. "Do you really think this is going to work?"

"I do," she enthused. "And it's too late to back out now, anyway. Everything is all set up, and you've got all your officers decorating the break room as we speak."

Jones scratched the stubble on his chin. "I know, but you must understand why I have reservations about this. We've suddenly decided to have this fundraiser, ostensibly to make the police look good while raising money for charity, and we've invited all the prominent members of the town. It's a little strange to begin with."

"The timeline is a bit short, I have to admit, but you've been over all the evidence yourself. I've spent my time talking to people and looking things up at the library.

Paired up with the information that you have, I know we're on the right track." As soon as she had finalized her notes, Sammy had brought everything down to the sheriff's office. He had listened patiently, and she could tell he was just waiting for his moment to tell her to go back to baking cookies, but by the end of her little presentation he had pulled out his file on Maureen Bradshaw and started collaborating with her.

Unfortunately, her idea for finalizing it all didn't sit well with him. "But this isn't how we normally do things," Jones explained. "We bring people in for questioning, talk to witnesses, gather concrete evidence. It's all by the book. I could send my boys out and probably find some clues that you missed—no offense—and get this taken care of without all the deception."

"I know, but I don't think that's going to work this time. Maureen's killer is out there, and this is a good way to gather all the suspects without giving them any reason to feel strange about being here. Do you have everyone in place?"

"I do," he replied begrudgingly.

"Just trust me, okay? If nothing else, you'll have a very nice Christmas party for the community. Let's go." She straightened the skirt of her dark green dress and headed for the break room, the heavy bootsteps of Sheriff Jones right behind her.

Several of their special guests had already arrived. There were only a few people that they needed to have here in order to make this work, and the rest would show up after they had Maureen's killer behind bars. The last thing they wanted was to embarrass the innocent. A large donation box for toys had been set up near the door. An officer was just putting the star on the top of the fluffy Christmas tree in the corner, and centerpieces had been set up on every table. Jones had questioned the location for this event, stating that it wasn't a big enough or nice enough space for a holiday charity fundraiser, but Sammy had argued that there was no time to secure another place. And while this wasn't as nice of a setting as the rec center, it would do just fine.

Carly Anderson had just arrived. In a pink dress and a rope of pearls, she looked like a happy homemaker as she carried in several trays of cupcakes. "Oh, Sammy! I didn't realize you would be here! I can't tell you how excited I was to receive an invitation to cater this fundraiser. I've been working on improving my skills, just like we talked about. I think you'll be pleased with these cupcakes."

"I can't wait to try them," Sammy assured her.

Next came Andrew Herzog, who looked rather proud of himself as he fiddled with the buttons on his suit jacket and found a seat at one of the front tables. Sammy scurried over to greet him. "I'm so glad you could make it, Mr. Herzog."

"Well, of course! It's not every day you get a special invitation because of your outstanding contributions to the community. I know that some people have opposed my developments, but it's good to see that the logical minds have prevailed. Have you had a chance to look over the plans for the new restaurant with your partner?"

"I did," Sammy admitted, "but she's not sure she wants something that big or that fancy. We'll talk about it some more, and I'll get back to you." She had shown the plans to Helen, who had laughed at them as Sammy had expected.

"There's no way I could operate a place like that," Helen had chuckled. "I wouldn't even know where to find the silverware."

"As soon as you say the word, I can get things going on it," Herzog promised. "I have a few bankers in my pocket, so it'll be no problem to get the property, tear down that old building, and break ground on the new one. Oh, and I forgot to give you the name of that marketing guy I know. I'm afraid I don't have any of his business cards on me."

The poor man had fallen completely for her scheme, and it made Sammy feel guilty. But she had to do this to get justice for Maureen, and she wasn't really hurting anyone so much as she was wasting a little bit of their time. "You can just email me the information when you get a chance."

The Radical Grandmas were the next to show up, and they whispered excitedly to each other as they walked in the door. "This is so exciting," Agnes said as she wrapped an arm around Sammy. "It's like something straight out of a movie."

"Be quiet, Agnes," Viola warned. "Someone is going to overhear you."

"I didn't say anything that would give it away," the blonde woman argued. "And I know you're jut as excited as I am."

"We all are," Linda amended, "but we need to behave ourselves and let Sammy do her job. Sammy dear, tell us where we're supposed to sit."

"Right there." Sammy pointed to a round table that was front and center to where a makeshift staging area had been set up on one side of the room right in front of a wall of windows. Puffy flakes of snow drifted slowly downward on the scenery outside, and Sammy realized this could become an annual event—minus tracking down a murderer, of course.

Just as the Grandmas got settled, Mr. McLaughlin came through the front door.

"I'm so glad you could come, and I can't tell you how much we appreciate what you're doing," Sammy said as she took several packages from the store manager. "These are going to bring in a good amount of money on auction."

"I couldn't really turn it down when Sheriff Jones called me personally, and I can afford to donate a few things from the store if it's going to benefit needy kids during the cold season. Plus, I think bringing along Santa to help with the auction was a great idea." He turned to the man he had brought in with him and patted him on the shoulder of his Santa suit.

Santa nodded but said nothing behind his fake beard.

"I'll get these set up on the table, and you two have a seat. Things will be getting started shortly."

"Thanks again, Ms. Baker." Mr. McLaughlin smiled, apparently having forgotten their awkward conversation, and sat down at the table next to the Radical Grandmas.

Sammy's stomach fluttered nervously. She knew this was the right thing to do, and it was the best way to find Maureen's killer. There wasn't a single piece of evidence she hadn't covered with Sheriff Jones, and while he might be reserved about the pretense of the party, he had completely agreed with her as to who the killer was. And Sammy had to admit that the idea of confronting the murderer face-to-face was scary, but she knew the sheriff and his brave men and women were all around her. She had to have faith in them and in God to keep her safe, because she was doing the right thing.

With a final look around the room, Sammy looked at Sheriff Jones and nodded. The doors to the break room were closed, two officers stationed in front of them. A few of the guests turned around to look, and Sammy tried to ignore them as she went to the front of the room. Her palms were sweaty as she clasped her hands in front of her and smiled at the small audience.

"As we wait for the rest of our guests to arrive, I just wanted to thank those of you who are here for everything you have done to contribute toward this fundraiser. Sunny Cove is a wonderful town, but sadly there are some children who are left behind. They will benefit from the generous donations that you have brought tonight."

A straggling round of applause went through the room, mostly headed up by the Grandmas.

"I would also like to take a moment to remember Maureen Bradshaw, who would have been delighted to be here tonight. Maureen was a spunky, energetic woman who was always interested in helping people, and I have no doubt that she would have jumped right in to help plan this fundraiser. Sadly, she was taken away from us far too soon, and I suppose it's no small secret that her death wasn't an accident."

The guests looked unsettled, but Sammy had expected that. She stepped away from the front of the room and began walking amongst the tables. "It's interesting that when you start looking for a killer, you begin to see numerous people who could have done the deed. You find reasons to suspect them, good solid reason that are hard to refute. People who might otherwise seem innocent suddenly seem capable of doing such a thing, such as Carly Anderson." She paused in front of the table where Carly sat.

Her face paled, and she looked as though she was about to pass out. "Me?" she squeaked. "I wouldn't hurt anybody."

"Maybe not," Sammy agreed, "but you have to admit that your behavior the night of the fundraiser was rather odd. You were hanging out by the Christmas puddings far longer than anyone else who had come to get a slice of dessert. Maureen's throat was swollen, and everyone knew she was allergic to nuts. You might not have appreciated the fact that my baking business seemed to take customers away from you, and it would have been an easy task for you to slip a nut into one of the puddings and let me take the blame."

"But...but I didn't!" she exclaimed, one hand coming to her mouth. "I wouldn't even dream of doing such a thing."

"Then would you care to explain what you were doing that night?" Sammy had a feeling she already knew, and she hated to embarrass the woman, but putting these people in the hot seat was going to be the best way to get the truth.

Carly hung her head. "I was very jealous that you had been asked to do the desserts. It was bound to be one of the biggest events of the season and very good for your business, but you already do so well. I know nothing about making Christmas puddings. I was just looking at them, trying to figure out how you made them, but..."

"Yes?" Sammy urged softly.

"I stole one," she admitted glumly. "It was a terrible thing to do in any case, but especially at a Christmas fundraiser! But I thought I could figure out the recipe and start making them on my own. I was sure you had found out and that was why you showed up at my bakery, and then I felt even worse when you offered to help me."

Sammy laid a hand on her shoulder. "If there's anything you ever need, all you have to do is ask. Those puddings were a challenge, and I'd be happy to share the recipe later."

The baker smiled up at her through her tears and nodded.

"That crosses one person off the list." Sammy took several steps across the room, sliding past the Grandmas. "But it turns out that Ms. Anderson wasn't the only one with a secret to hide. Mr. McLaughlin could have just as easily had something to do with Maureen's death."

The store manager's face turned a dangerous shade of red. "How dare you accuse me of such a thing?" he asked. "I wouldn't hurt a soul."

"But Maureen knew that your specialty Christmas items had come from a sweatshop," Sammy pointed out. "She made a big scene in your store and very likely cut into those precious holiday profits. That had to make you very angry."

"It did," Mr. McLaughlin admitted, "but I was more angry with myself than with her. I was the one who had ordered that shipment of cheap clothing, only thinking about making money and not who might be hurt in the process. I should have looked into the clothing more before I ordered it."

"So you weren't so angry with Maureen that you strangled her at the fundraiser and threw her in the pool?"

"Absolutely not! In fact, I ended up donating the entire lot and taking a loss. The items had already been made, so there was no point in throwing them away, but at least this way someone gets some use out of them."

Sammy smiled at him, glad that he had seen the error of his ways. She believed him when he said that he had nothing to do with Maureen's death. He was a good man at heart. "I'm sure there will be quite a few people who will really appreciate that."

Sheriff Jones cleared his throat and stepped forward. "With all due respect, Ms. Baker, I think that's about enough. The police department is doing everything it can to find Mrs. Bradshaw's killer."

She smiled at him, grateful that he had not only remembered his role in this charade but that he was willing to carry it out. "Would you like to tell us about one of your main pieces of evidence?"

He tucked his thumbs into his belt. "As I'm sure everyone saw, there was a rather large set of wet boot prints that led away from the scene of the crime."

"And about what size would you say they were?"

"About a thirteen or so," he replied, "but I'm not sure what that has to do with any of this."

Sammy nodded. "That's a fairly large shoe size. It would take a tall man to wear a boot like that, someone like Andrew Herzog, perhaps?" She turned to the land developer.

He put his hand in the air, palms out. "Now, just hold on a

CHRISTMAS PUDS & KILLERS

second. I thought I was being brought here because of what I've done for Sunny Cove, not to get falsely accused of murder."

"But you did have an argument with Maureen at the rec center fundraiser, and the two of you had been battling over the piece of property that the land sits on."

Mr. Herzog gave her annoyed look. "Yes, that's true, but I would never hurt a woman, and especially not an older woman like Maureen."

"Then would you care to tell us what size shoe you wear?" Sammy asked.

He pressed his lips together so hard that the skin around them turned white. "Thirteen," he finally answered.

"Well, there we have it. Matching shoe sizes, a motive, and he was even at the scene of the crime. What more could we need?" Sammy spread her hands in finality.

"Now wait just a minute!" Mr. Herzog was on his feet, towering over her. Sheriff Jones took a step forward, but Sammy wasn't intimidated, not this time. "It's true that Maureen and I didn't get along very well, but I had come to that fundraiser so I could try to see her side of things. I had been complaining about the deal to my wife, and she convinced me that I should go to the rec center and try to understand why she wanted so badly to save it. I hardly even had a chance to look around before the old biddy picked a fight with me just because I was there. I can see why she did, and I can't really blame her, but I left as soon as the argument was over."

"Mr. Herzog, you can have a seat," Sammy said calmly as she returned to the front of the room and addressed the crowd as a whole once again. "I suppose that just leaves us with two other pieces of evidence, one of which comes from Mrs. Linda Travelstead. Linda, would you care to tell us what you remember about the night of the fundraiser?"

"Quite a bit," she replied proudly. "I may be up there in my years, but my old brain still works like a steel trap. But what stood out to me the most was the number of Santas who were there."

"Oh," Sammy replied. "I guess you're talking about the waitstaff. It was a rather nice effect, don't you think?"

Linda shook her head, her jewelry glittering. "No, I'm afraid it wasn't. You see, there were seven Santas when we arrived, but only six later in the evening. I would know. I used to be an accountant, and it's all about the numbers to me."

"I see. And who knows more about being Santa than Santa himself?" Sammy pointed across the room, where the Santa from Gibb's was slowly sidling toward a side exit.

He stopped in his tracks and shook his padded belly. "Ho ho ho! Now, now. We wouldn't want to accuse Santa of being on the naughty list. I wasn't even there that night."

CHRISTMAS PUDS & KILLERS

"But you're the only other one in this room that could fill the boots that left those prints," Sammy pointed out.

"Then perhaps you can explain why Maureen had this article about a master of disguise who had posed as a security guard and robbed the hotel in Oak Hills last year? The same hotel where she had been staying when she was robbed? The police never caught him, but they suspected that he pulled this scam on a regular basis to steal from his employers." Sammy produced the wrinkled article from the pocket of her dress. With Viola's help, she had found the original article in the library archives, one that hadn't been nearly ruined by pool water and was much easier to read.

"There's no proof that I was involved in either that crime or this one," Santa objected, taking another cautious step toward the door.

Mr. McLaughlin was on his feet now, looking back and forth between Sammy and Santa. "Maureen had approached me just before the fundraiser," he said in a trembling voice. "I thought at first she was just going to yell at me about the cheap clothing again, but instead she said she wanted to talk to me about issues with some of my temporary staff. She mentioned something about a newspaper clipping."

"And that could also explain why Maureen was so upset about the waitstaff being dressed up like they were," Sammy asserted. "She already suspected this man, and the red suits made her rather uncomfortable."

Santa made a run for it. The police officers jumped to action, but the other guests at the party got to him first. Mr. Herzog easily blocked the door with his large frame. Viola and Agnes grabbed Santa's toy sack and whipped it over his head, while Linda grabbed the back of his jacket and dug in her heels. The cops soon had him in their custody with shiny silver handcuffs slapped on his wrists.

"All right. Let's take that beard off," Sheriff Jones commanded.

One of the other officers removed the white fluff, revealing numerous scratches on his cheeks.

"What's that all about?" Jones asked.

"It's from wearing this silly beard all day every day," the man protested. "It's giving me a rash."

"No way," Agnes asserted, shaking a fist in the air at him. "I saw you the night of the fundraiser, looking all scraggly with your skinny legs and your big boots and bits of fluff stuck to your face. I thought you were homeless, and I was going to ask you to come in and enjoy the food with us. But by the time I got outside, you had run off into the night."

Santa's shoulders slumped. "Fine. You caught me. I was posing as the store Santa with a plan to rob the place once everyone went home. I'd been taking a little every night, and this was going to be my last shift. I didn't expect Mr. McLaughlin to ask me to extend my shift by a couple of hours to come here, but I figured it wouldn't matter since I wasn't in costume."

"And my assistant manager has just informed me that his locker is full of jewelry and electronics," the store manager confirmed, sliding his cell phone back in his jacket pocket. "None of it was purchased."

Sheriff Jones had fished the man's wallet out of his pants pocket and was studying his driver's license. "Darrell Burns, you're under arrest for the murder of Maureen Bradshaw and for stealing goods from Gibb's Department Store."

10

HAVE A MERRY CHRISTMAS

Viola's house was one that befitted a former librarian. While she had a proper study lined with bookshelves, every room in the house seemed to have books in it. They were either on a shelf amidst knickknacks, stacked on a table, or proudly presented as a focal piece on the mantel. It was her turn to host the annual Radical Grandmas Christmas party, and Sammy had been invited to celebrate with them.

"I don't know that I can keep up with you ladies!" she laughed as she slumped down onto the couch after a rousing game of charades. "Between the songs, the dancing, and the games, I don't know where you get all your energy!"

"Straight from the good Lord himself," Agnes assured her with a smile. "If it weren't for our faith, we never would have made it through the trials and tribulations that made us who we are today. We might not have our husbands, and many of our families are far away, but we always have each other and Jesus."

"You're very lucky," Sammy said with a smile.

"We think so, too," Linda agreed. "And we're also very lucky that we've had you come into our lives. As devastating as it was to lose Maureen, I really felt like I was alive again while we were tracking down her killer. You did most of the work, of course, but it was exhilarating nonetheless."

"To be honest with you, I feel bad about deceiving some of those people. Granted, we did have the rest of the guests come in for the youth fundraiser at the police station, so that wasn't a complete lie. And I really will refer some business to Carly. The cupcakes she brought were wonderful! But what about Mr. Herzog? He took all that time and trouble to plan out a new building for Just Like Grandma's, and I know full well that we won't be having him build it."

"Don't even think about it," Agnes said with a laugh. "I happen to know that he's been trying to sell that exact plan for the past year! He's presented it to every restaurant and store that has even considered coming to his county. You didn't waste any of his time, dear."

Sammy felt a certain sense of peace in knowing this. Maureen's killer had been found, the stolen goods from Gibb's had been returned, Carly had improved her business, Mr. McLaughlin had learned a good lesson, and the most recent news they had received was that the

Sunny Cove Recreation Center would be remodeled and kept open. "I'm so glad to hear that."

"Now it's present time!" Linda announced.

"Oh, I didn't know we were exchanging gifts!" Sammy exclaimed, feeling embarrassed.

"Well, we aren't. But the three of us wanted to get you a little something to thank you for everything you've done for us." Viola winked as she picked up a large box from under the tree and handed it to Sammy.

It was heavy, and she pulled away the ribbon with shaking fingers. Inside was an item that looked something like a bucket with a lid that clamped down over the top. "A vintage pudding mold! How wonderful!" Sammy laughed. "After the fundraiser, I hadn't thought I would make another pudding again. But now I'll have to."

Later that afternoon, when Sammy finally went home for the night with the pudding mold riding safely on the passenger floorboard, she looked up at the star shining brightly in the deep blue December sky. "Thank you, God, for bringing these ladies to me. I couldn't have asked for a better gift."

Thank you so much for reading, *Rolling Out a Mystery*. We hope you really enjoyed the story. If so, leaving a review is a great way to let others know (reviews are such a great encouragement to our authors also!). Leave a Review Now!

Also, make sure to sign up to receive PureRead Donna Doyle updates at PureRead.com for more great mysteries, exclusive offers and news of our new releases. We love to surprise our readers and would love to have you as part of our reader family!

Much love, and thanks again,

Your Friends at PureRead

* * *

Sign Up For Updates:

http://pureread.com/donnadoyle

BROWSE ALL OF DONNA DOYLE'S BOOKS

http://pureread.com/donnadoylebooks

MORE BAKER'S DOZEN MYSTERIES...

Dying For Cupcakes

Rolling Out a Mystery

BOXSET READING ENJOYMENT

ENJOY HOURS OF CLEAN READING WITH SOME OF OUR BESTSELLING BOXSETS...

Here at PureRead we love to offer great stories and great value to our readers. We have a growing library of amazing clean read boxsets that deliver dozens of delightful stories in every bundle. Here are just a few, or browse them all and grab a bargain on our website...

Look for PureRead titles on Amazon or visit our website at
PureRead.com/boxsets

PureRead Clean Reads Box Set Volume II

PureRead Clean Reads Box Set Volume I

PureRead Christmas Stocking of Stories

Seasons of Regency Romance Boxset

PureRead Terri Grace Legacy Boxset

Rainbow Mountain Brides Boxset

Mega Amish Romance Boxset

Christian Love 21 Book Contemporary Romance Boxset

** BROWSE ALL OF OUR BOX SETS **

http://PureRead.com/boxsets

FREE TO JOIN...

DON'T FORGET TO SIGN UP FOR
UPDATES (100% FREE TO JOIN)

Sign up for updates and be the the first to hear about new
releases, special offers and more from Donna Doyle and
our other clean and cozy mystery authors...

Go to http://pureread.com/donnadoyle

ABOUT PUREREAD

T hank you for reading!

Here at PureRead we aim to serve you, our dear reader, with good, clean Christian stories. You can be assured that any PureRead book you pick up will not only be hugely enjoyable, but free of any objectionable content.

We are deeply thankful to you for choosing our books. Your support means that we can continue to provide stories just like the one you have just read.

PLEASE LEAVE A REVIEW

Please do consider leaving a review for this book on Amazon - something as simple as that can help others just like you discover and enjoy the books we publish, and your reviews are a constant encouragement to our hard working writers.

LIKE OUR PUREREAD FACEBOOK PAGE

Love Facebook? We do too and PureRead has a very special Facebook page where we keep in touch with readers.

To like and follow PureRead on Facebook go to **Facebook.com/pureread**

OUR WEBSITE

To browse all of our PureRead books visit our website at PureRead.com

Made in the USA
Middletown, DE
09 May 2019